The Empress' New Hair

By S.F. Hardy

Illustrator: Shanaya Ellsberry, SOS Graphic Designs.com
Cover Design: Shanaya Ellsberry, SOS Graphic Designs.com

Published by G Publishing, LLC

ISBN: 978-0-9849360-9-0

Library of Congress Control Number: 2012943217

Printed in the United States of America

Happening right now in a land near and dear Empress Zaina Niara of Detroit Charm speaks to her mirror with distress and fear.

"Mirror, Mirror on the wall, how can I possibly rule the empire when my curls continue to fall? Everyone knows that every tress must be in place! They will all laugh at my unruly hair thinking I must have no grace. No matter the coiffure it gives me problems and not the flair an empress is supposed to have when it comes to her hair."

Coiffure: a style or manner of arranging the hair.

"By permission. From *Merriam-Webster's Collegiate® Dictionary, Eleventh Edition©2012* by Merriam-Webster, Incorporated (http://www.merriam-webster.com/)."

"Now, now Empress, slow down dear, didn't your mom and aunt teach you to embrace your hair?"

"Well, yes mirror— they constantly tell me that like the world my hair is diverse and to spend no time worrying about such small superficial things— as there are much bigger matters to concern myself with in this huge universe."

"I know you don't want to hear it Empress, but they are telling you best."

"Yes, this may be true, which is why I want hair that is no maintenance. I've tried:
braids,
sisterlocks,
short hair,
long hair,
naturally curly hair,
blow-dried straight,
and even twist, but none of these options offer me a permanent no maintenance, don't have to do my hair—EVERY DAY
fix."

Embrace: to take up readily or gladly b. cherish, love.

Diverse: differing from one another: UNLIKE <people with diverse interests>.

"By permission. From *Merriam-Webster's Collegiate® Dictionary, Eleventh Edition©2012* by Merriam-Webster, Incorporated (http://www.merriam-webster.com/)."

"The sisterlocks wouldn't lock and like the twist, shortly after getting them they would only prove rebellious and simply unravel in resistance."

Sisterlocks: very small uniformed twists that mature into permanent locks.

"The long hair seems to be even a bigger bother; I only wear it long because of the demands of my father."

"The blow-dried hair would get frizzy in the humid air; this silly hair of mines is far from fair."

"I seemed to like my short hair the best, but even it had to be maintained often, as after a week or so it too became a mess."

"Sometimes, I wear my hair in a bun. Although convenient, timeless and elegant, they are also plain and not always so fun— unless it's a chignon."

Chignon: a knot of hair worn at the back of the head.

"The curly hair always turns into a big ole poof and has to be shampooed and conditioned every day! Tell me mirror, why does it seem that no matter what I do to my hair, it just gets in my way?"

"Empress, have you ever considered that maybe, just maybe, you aren't supposed to wear your hair in any one style— that you have been bestowed with hair that is extremely versatile?"

Versatile: having many uses or <u>applications</u> <versatile building material>

As the empress sat in the mirror and continued to pout, some faux hairstylists also known as kitchen beauticians were in the royal court, roaming about.

Overhearing the empress' seemingly small dilemma, and being opportunist, they decided to take advantage of the situation and present the empress with a solution that would make them rich.

"Oh Empress Zaina how do you do? Wait— let usssss— answer that for you. Not good from what we hear, but we have a solution especially for you, so do not fear."

"Empress you change your hair every week. Why haven't you found a style that is becoming of you that you don't have to constantly tweak? You are an empress and should sport your hair as such. We will design a style for you and only you that no one else will be able to wear or touch."

Faux: imitation.

"By permission. From *Merriam-Webster's Collegiate® Dictionary, Eleventh Edition©2012* by Merriam-Webster, Incorporated (http://www.merriam-webster.com/)."

"Well, I guess I like them all, but I get bored and frustrated with them quickly," Empress Zaina shrugged.

"Honestly my dear, as the Empress of Detroit Charm, you must flaunt one hairstyle and one hairstyle only."

"Before we can create a couture style for you to display, you must pay us lots of money to make your hair this way."

As the empress sat and pondered the kitchen beauticians' proposal, her mommy and auntie walked in as if they could smell trouble.

Couture: the business of designing, making, and selling fashionable custom-made women's clothing.

"Empress you mustn't let these imposters touch your hair! You don't know their credentials and not to mention your aunt and I believe that they couldn't possibly care— about you or our community, let alone your hair. Money is their motive, not the care or treatment of you or your hair," cried Empress Zaina's mommy dear."

Not knowing what the imposters truly had in mind auntie also felt personally inclined to express what was on her mind.

"Empress you must not listen to this nonsense. Accept and be happy with your hair and its ability to be diverse. You have to set an example for the people of the empire. If you wear your hair in one style how can we expect others to accept differences among the community? It is your responsibility as empress to create unity through diversity!"

"Hey guys please don't fret, I'm sure that with these stylists good treatment is what I surely will get— everything they have to offer and finally, for once, my hair will no longer be a bother."

Credentials: something that gives a title to credit or confidence; also: QUALIFICATION.

"By permission. From *Merriam-Webster's Collegiate® Dictionary, Eleventh Edition©2012* by Merriam-Webster, Incorporated (http://www.merriam-webster.com/)."

The next day against her mommy and auntie's wishes, Empress Zaina was getting her hair done in the royal kitchen among the pots, pans and dirty dishes.

When it was all complete, she got out of the chair, going to her trusty mirror so that she could see her hair.

"Oh my gosh!" Empress screamed in despair. "What have you two done to my hair?!!!!!"

"We simply did what you asked— we GOT RID of your hair!"

Despair: to lose all hope or confidence.

As she looked at her tendrils all over the floor she began to shout, "I asked for a permanent fix!" Pointing to what looked like a buzz cut, she screamed "NOT THIS!"

"I want my hair and money back as stated in your guarantee!"

"Well, you see Empress, it stated in the fine print you have to catch us first to get your money back! As for your hair— Hummmmmm, that's another story," the kitchen beauticians said in unison as they began to run.

A chase ensued through the royal court out into the community where the citizens awaited to see Empress Zaina's new hair.

"Wait! Come back…" Empress Zaina shouted in despair, "This is not fair! I never told you two that I wanted to get rid of my hair!"

The faces of the people were of awe and shock. The adults afraid to be honest praised the empress' new hair. But the children were different, questioning the adults about the empress' hair.

"What hair? We don't see any hair what happened to it, did it just disappear?"

Hearing what the people were saying made the empress run faster but she could not catch the imposters and she was soon short of breath. After a while she had no choice but to stop and rest.

After five long minutes of sitting, the empress still had not been able to catch her breath, when everything starts to get dark and blurry. Suddenly, the empress finds herself in her royal bed only to discover she had just awoken from a very bad dream.

"Mirror, Mirror! WAKE UP, WAKE UP! I just had a nightmare that seemed so real."

Empress proceeded to tell the mirror about her dream.

"Well Empress, maybe now you understand that having the same hairstyle is not as good as it seems."

"Mirror, I don't think I will regret this when I say, I have learned my lesson: to accept and embrace that I can wear my hair in many different ways. My hair was made like this for a reason and I will happily wear my hair different for each and every season. I will change my hair every day, maintenance and all, and when I want advice on my hair there are only two very special trustworthy people I will call, Mommy and Auntie!"

The End

CPSIA information can be obtained
at www.ICGtesting.com
Printed in the USA
LVHW072226140521
687203LV00002BB/55